W9-BWN-701

THEODORE BIKEL'S

THE CITY OF LIGHT

Aimee Ginsburg Bikel

Illustrations by Noah Phillips

MOMENTBOOKS

MANDEL VILAR PRESS

This book is typeset in Walbaum MT.
The paper used in this book meets the minimum requirements of ANSI/NISO Z39.48-1992 (R1997). ∞

Book design by Sophie Appel

Cover design by Nadine Epstein
and Anne Masters

Cover illustration by Noah Phillips

MomentBooks
4115 Wisconsin Ave LL10, NW Washington DC 20016
momentbooks.com | momentmag.com

Mandel Vilar Press
19 Oxford Court
Simsbury, Connecticut 06070
americasforconservation.org | mvpress.org

Publisher's Cataloging-in-Publication Data

Names: Bikel, Theodore, author.
Title: The City of Light / Theodore Bikel & Aimee Ginsburg Bikel; Illustrations by Noah Phillips.
Description: Washington, DC: MomentBooks; Simsbury, Connecticut: Mandel Vilar Press, [2019] | An expanded, illustrated version of the story originally published in Moment Magazine, December 2014. | Interest age level: 10 and up.
Identifiers: ISBN 9781942134619 (lithocase hardcover)
Subjects: LCSH: Bikel, Theodore—Childhood and youth—Juvenile literature. | Jews-—Austria—Vienna—Biography—Juvenile literature. | Antisemitism—Austria—Vienna—History—20th century—Juvenile literature. | Hanukkah—Juvenile literature. | Light—Religious aspects—Judaism— Juvenile literature. | Kristallnacht, 1938—Juvenile literature. | Holocaust Jewish—Holocaust survivors | CYAC: Bikel, Theodore—Childhood and youth. | Jews—Austria—Vienna—Biography. | Antisemitism—Austria—Vienna—History—20th century. | Hanukkah. | Light—Religious aspects—Judaism. | Holocaust Jewish—Holocaust survivors.
Classification: LCC DS135.
A93 B55 2019 | DDC
940.5318092—dc23

Printed in Canada
19 20 21 22 23 24 25 26 27 / 9 8 7 6 5 4 3 2 1

In loving memory of
Mirriam and Joseph Bikel

And to Wolfie, Freya,
Auggie, Imogen Rita, and
Clark Theodore Bikel.
Grandpa Theo loved you
with all of his heart.

Foreword

Once upon a time lived a marvelous man named Theodore Bikel. He was a famous actor and a singer who was full of goodness and joy. He laughed a lot and loved singing and playing his guitar. If you ask your grandparents or maybe even your parents about him, they'll probably say they saw him on TV, in the movies, or in the theater, and maybe they heard some of his records. Theo loved being Jewish and worked hard to make this world a better place for all people everywhere.

He always told a lot of stories about the interesting things that happened to him during his long and wonderful life. Most of his stories were funny; sometimes they were sad. The older he became, the more he told stories from when he was a small boy, back in his birthplace: the city of Vienna, in a country called Austria. At that time, his name was Te'o, the German nickname for "Theodore." There was one memory that he loved best of all. In this special memory, Te'o is doing one of his favorite things: exploring the Vienna Woods with his mama (Mirriam) and his papa (Joseph). Even though the woods were only about an hour away from the city, going there was always a special occasion. Mama, with her cloth bag of delicious sandwiches, red cherries, sweet marzipan, and a thermos of hot tea, would settle down on the checkered blanket and prepare their picnic. Young Te'o and Papa walked along the trails, singing loudly in German, Yiddish, and Hebrew. They sang Jewish songs, songs about building a beautiful new country for the Jewish people, and songs about a better world for all working people, everywhere. "Never forget these things," Papa would tell him. "They are the most important." After their picnic, chilled from the wind and the damp of the earth, they would stop at the inn at the edge of the woods for a bowl of chicken soup with liver dumplings. The innkeeper always smiled at young Te'o and gave him a few extra dumplings so he would "grow to be big and strong."

Te'o could not imagine the horrors that would come so soon. He could not imagine that almost overnight their neighbors, his teachers, even the innkeeper, would become enemies, full of hatred and malice, simply because he was a Jewish boy. He could not imagine that he and his parents would have to leave his darling *Oma* (grandmother) behind when they escaped from Vienna. They got out just in the nick of time, right before the borders were closed, and no Jews were allowed to leave. Even though Papa and Mama had tried with all of their might, they could not get an extra exit permit for Oma. "I am old and Te'o is still young," Oma said. "You must go now and take my Te'o to safety before it is too late." They were only allowed to take one suitcase each. How much can you possibly fit into one suitcase? During the voyage across the Mediterranean Sea, they felt excited about their new life but heartbroken that they had to leave so much behind—worst of all Oma, but also their friends, their beloved books, and most of the things they had owned. Then, two miracles happened. Oma, through her cleverness and courage, was able to save all their belongings. And, once the little family reached their new home, they were able to get a permit for Oma. Soon she joined them in their little house in Tel Aviv, and their precious belongings arrived in a great big wooden crate.

As you now know, little Te'o grew up to be the world famous Mr. Theodore Bikel. He was truly grateful for his good, happy life. And yet, deep inside, he was often sad. He never really forgot the sorrow and the fright of having to escape from his happy childhood in Vienna. He never forgot the horror of having to leave behind his beloved books and his friends and worst of all his Oma. He could never forget that even though his own story had a happy ending, the story did not end happily for many of the Jews of Vienna and all of Austria and Europe. When he thought about this, it made his heart ache, and he tried to make himself happy again by singing and playing his guitar.

Theo also knew that now, today, in our time and right here in our own neighborhoods or very nearby, so many people, especially children, live without enough food, love, or safety. These thoughts might have made him bitter and angry, or full of despair. But, instead, the light in his heart gave him the strength to fight for what is right, and to help other people have better lives.

"I know what happens when good people stay silent when they see bad things happening," he used to say. "I promise I will always speak up and cry out when things are unjust and people are suffering, never mind what religion, color, or gender they may be. All men and women are my brothers and sisters." What better way is there to fill up our world—our cities—with light?

THE CITY OF LIGHT

SWEET CAKES

The boy was thirteen. The city he lived in was all light—a city of waltzes, of sweet confections. Through the windows of the coffeehouses on every corner of every lane he watched the intellectuals debate and play chess, and although he was too young to take his place among them, it was a foregone conclusion that his time would come.

The boy was a Jew, and he liked his people and their stories, their legends, and their mysteries. The small apartment that he lived in with his papa, mama, and Oma was full of books about Jewish kings and queens, fantastic journeys, and a magical burning bush. His favorite book was small, very old, and covered in red leather. It told the tales of long-ago heroes like Judah the Maccabee and his brothers. An only child, the boy liked reading these stories at bedtime and would fall asleep imagining he was part of those adventures.

The Jews in the city lived well; they were the merchants and the lawyers, the doctors and the writers, the playwrights, the artists. As far as the boy could tell, there were several kinds of Jews in the city. There were those who looked different from everyone else, who wore different clothes and whose language—Yiddish—had the unmistakable lilt of Eastern European languages. They all lived close to each other and to the houses of prayer they would walk to on Sabbath and holidays. They reminded the boy of his *Zayde* (grandfather) who lived in a village in the countryside, a two-day train ride from Vienna. Zayde had a little red beard, he made jokes that the boy didn't always understand, and when he sang the Sabbath blessings, he sounded like some kind of an angel.

There were other Jews in the city; they were not like his Zayde at all. They spoke in High German and wore stylish clothes, and their heads were uncovered. They looked like their non-Jewish neighbors in every way. These Jews lived all over the city, and they were known for their great music and art, their new ideas, and their inventions.

The boy's family lived like these other Jews, in one of the city's many neighborhoods. But his papa spoke to him in the Jewish language, Yiddish. And on the holidays, Mama and Oma made special food, and Papa prayed with a voice as beautiful as Zayde's. After the meal, with the crumbs still on the table, Papa would read stories from their books, some quite sad and some very funny. Then, sipping from the sweet sticky wine in the large silver cup, he would speak about the coming time when they would have their own country, and when all men and women of the world would live in peace, equality, and safety like real brothers and sisters.

On Chanukah, there were even more songs and stories, about courage and miracles, and Oma made her special latkes. On these special evenings, surrounded by the light of the *chanukiya* (menorah) and the love of his family, the boy felt especially happy.

From time to time, Papa took the boy to visit the *Stadttempel*, the old and grand temple by the river. It was a wondrous place. The boy never tired of going there, running his fingers on the smooth polished wood, and listening to the beautiful music. He especially loved looking at the *ner tamid*, the eternal flame glowing above the Holy Ark. The rabbi told them that the eternal flame shows us that our spirit can never die, and that goodness and truth will always light our way. It seemed to him that this eternal flame must be the secret source of power illuminating his beloved city.

But not all was well in the City of Light. The boy's mama and papa had told him about anti-Semitism. Sometimes, the gentile boys in his classroom yelled out insults and taunts about Jews killing Christ, and about being dirty. Why are they doing that? the boy thought. They know I didn't kill anybody, and they can see that I am very clean. He tried to understand it, but it just didn't make any sense. The City of Light could not live without its Jews, and the city knew it. The boy knew that people looked up to the Jews as much as they looked down on them. He could tell that the people of the city actually admired the Jews in many ways, and this made him feel proud, but also nervous because he understood that with the admiration there was also envy, and that sometimes envy turned to hate, so that you could never be sure of where you stood.

The boy had his Bar Mitzvah. It was a modest affair held in a *shtibel*, the small and simple looking prayer house that his father preferred over the grand Stadttempel by the river. This congregation was made up of mostly old Polish Jews—not very old-fashioned or religious like Zayde—but not too modern either. The men all listened in wonderment as the boy delivered his Bar Mitzvah speech in crisp modern Hebrew; this was the gift of his father, who wanted his son to speak this old-new language of their people, not only the language of the Jews in the city. After the prayers and his speech came the mazel tovs, a sweet wine *kiddush* and honey cake baked by his Oma.

Later, at home, there were some presents, books mostly, and a visit to the theater. That was it. The boy kept wondering what exactly had happened that supposedly turned him into a man. A *man*, a Jewish strong man, a hero like Judah Maccabee—that's what he thought he might be. Maybe he was not quite ready yet, but in his mind, the mind of a Jewish almost-man, these were the legends that nourished him and that gave him hope.

Every day, there were ominous signs of more trouble to come. From across the border, the dictator was spewing a daily litany of Jew-hatred, and an invasion was imminent. But life went on. The city waltzed, the city sang; sweet cakes were consumed by the ton, and in the coffeehouses, intellectuals played chess and debated politics, philosophy, and art. The high holidays came and went, then Succoth and Chanukah, and another chance to dream of Judah Maccabee, of Jews as victors instead of victims.

And then, it happened: the tanks and armored cars rumbled across the border, unstopped and unstoppable.

Within days, the boy saw elderly Jews spat upon and beaten; elderly women were forced to clean the sidewalks with their coats, and men were forced to scrub the streets with their toothbrushes. School reopened, and during the morning assembly, the principal made a speech in which he declared, "If in the first exuberance of joy, excesses should happen, we will not be inclined to prevent them." Sure enough, a few hours later, a group of the older boys burst into his classroom and asked the children to point out the Jewish students. The teacher stood silently as the boy and his nine Jewish classmates were dragged from the classroom and beaten. When he came home from school, bruised and bloody, his papa wept.

The terror grew. Every day brought new regulations, new burdens. They tried to adjust, shrink into the shadows, but there was no safety to be found. Their neighbors, who had always been perfectly polite and smiled at him when they saw him, had overnight turned into unfriendly, cold strangers who looked away, said nothing, and did nothing at all to try and stop what was happening. The boy, who only yesterday had felt himself to be an integral part of the city, knew he would never feel completely at home ever again.

Then came the night of horrors. Houses of worship, shtibels, and synagogues were smashed, sacred objects defiled, Torah scrolls torn and trampled on. And the Stadttempel, the beautiful, wondrous temple where his papa liked to take him from time to time, where the wood was so smooth and the *ner tamid* was supposed to glow eternally, was smashed and shattered.

Where, oh where, is Judah Maccabee now? Where is the liberator of my people? The boy wondered. But, even if he were to come, the eternal light was so thoroughly demolished that not even one drop of pure oil remained—the light could not be rekindled.

The devastation continued, proceeding from mayhem to murder, from town to town, from country to country; it seemed there was no way to stop it, and it would end.

SWEET CAKES
JUDE

One day the boy walked home and took a shortcut through the park, the same shortcut he had taken many times, but now the area was forbidden to Jews. He knew it was forbidden, but on this day he was a little tired, or maybe he had to hurry home for a Hebrew class, or to help his mama with some chores, or maybe he plain forgot. Some hooligans spotted him and started to chase him: "There goes one of them, let's get him!" they said. They almost caught up with him, but although he was not really good at sports, he ran for his life and made it home in one piece, pale, panting, and afraid.

That night the boy dreamed of a glorious rescue:

A band of brave and strong Maccabees, with Judah at the head, tall and golden with great locks of long black hair, had arrived in the city and brought redemption to the people. The boy watched with amazement and relief as the men, his men, his heroes, reconsecrated the temple and rekindled the ner tamid, the eternal flame. All at once, the temple was filled from edge to edge with a great and brilliant light.

The wonder of it made the boy smile in his sleep. But when he awoke, he was in the dark, back in the place of oppression. He realized that there had been no Maccabean liberation, and he wept.

It took many years and the combined might of several nations to subdue the tyrant. The joy over the victory was tempered by deep sadness; the losses had been too great to bear. Slowly, very slowly, some of the survivors made their way back to the city while others found homes in new lands and never returned; the memories were just too painful. Those who decided to return to the city built and restored what they could. But not everything that is broken can be mended.

Many years passed, and the boy, now an old man with grandchildren of his own, came back to visit the place of his youth: the city he remembered for its waltzes and sweet confections, but also for those things he did not like to think about. He saw that once more there was a community of Jews, once more there was life. The boy had had a very good life, full of music, love, and grand adventures. Just like his papa had wanted, he had tried to make the world a better place for everyone. But in all of the years after his escape from the City of Light, he never really felt at home again. The man stood for many moments on the street in front of the home, the building he had lived in with Mama, Papa and Oma, and looked up at his old home. In his imagination, he heard Papa singing the Sabbath prayers, and smelled Oma's honey cake fresh from the oven.

Then he went to see the Stadttempel. He stood at the doors of the temple, now restored to its former grandeur; then he entered and greeted the familiar places.

Everything seemed the same but for the eternal light. In place of the original, now hung a replica; yes, it was lit; yet there seemed to be no real light emanating from it. How could it remain extinguished after the barbarians had been defeated? Where was the glorious eternal flame, showing us that our spirit does not die, *cannot* die; that goodness and truth will always live on?

Suddenly, it was clear . . . the light was there. It had been there all the time! The ner tamid, the eternal flame, was in his own heart.

Az egmor beshir mizmor . . . The old man hummed the last line of the Chanukah song to himself. "I will conclude with a song of gratitude." Maybe we cannot fix everything that has been broken, but with our song and with our love, we can always find our way back to the light.

Afterword

"Not everything that has been broken can be mended," the story says. This is true. But one of the loveliest things about the people of our world is that we often *do* try to fix things that have been broken. When something breaks and we fix it, it might not ever go back to the way it was, but sometimes, something beautiful and new can come out of it. You have probably experienced this yourself in your own life.

Remember the part in the story about a terrible night when all of the windows of the Jewish shops were shattered, the synagogues destroyed, and the eternal light extinguished? This is something that really happened in Vienna, on November 9, 1938. It is known as *Kristallnacht*, which means "Night of Glass" in German. It was after this night that things became so terrible for the Jews who lived there that many did not survive.

Years went by, World War II came to an end, and the people who had only been children during Kristallnacht grew up and became adults. And as time went by, the people of Vienna, the younger ones as well as the older ones, felt more and more dismayed, regretful, and even ashamed about everything that had happened. They, or their parents, had let the worst possible things happen right there in their city and their country without stopping it. They knew that the people who had done the terrible things and the others who let it happen had been plain, normal people, living plain, normal lives. How could plain, normal people behave this way? Why had they listened to and believed all of the lies? Why had they blamed others for their own problems, simply because they were from a different religion or group? Why had they let their hearts fill up with so much hatred and fear? And how had they let fear and hatred take complete control of their lives, of their country?

The people of the City of Light didn't know how they could fix what had happened, but they wanted to be sure nothing like that could ever, ever happen again. They realized that, to make sure bad things don't happen again, they should try to understand them, never forget them, and talk about them a lot, even if it can be upsetting to think about bad things that happened. Even you might be feeling a little upset right now. That is understandable.

One person who worked hard to make Austria a good and safe country for everyone was a very wonderful woman named Barbara Prammer, the former president of the Austrian government. One of the things that was most important to her was to teach the children of Austria about equality and fairness, respect and cooperation between all people. She knew that if everyone understood how important it is to be kind to each other, everyone's lives would be better. One day, she had a special idea: she invited Theo to Vienna to sing his beautiful songs, as a way to remember what happened, to apologize, and to show honor and respect to all of those who had been hurt.

And so, on November 9, 2013, *exactly* seventy-five years after Kristallnacht, the Night of Glass, the Boy (Te'o), now an old man of almost ninety with beautiful white hair and a beautiful white beard, went back to Vienna with his guitar and his memories.

On that day, many of the important and powerful people of Austria came to the Parliament—the heart of the Austrian democracy—to hear Theo's singing. There were ministers, ambassadors, army commanders, council members, and many more leaders of the country—even the Prime Minister—and they all wanted to pay their respect to all of the Jewish people who were chased away, hurt, or killed. Theo, sitting next to his friend Merima Kljuco (who played the accordion when he sang), thanked everyone for inviting him to come, and for deciding to honor his people in this way. He told them that he still loved this city, the City of Lights of his childhood, where the music was so beautiful and the cakes in the cafés looked so pretty. Then he told them how sad and scared he had felt when he had to run away to save his life, and that he had felt like a refugee for the rest of his life, even though he loved his life and his new home in the United States. Everyone listened to him very seriously. These things were not so easy to hear, but they were very important anyway. Then Theo sang his favorite songs for them, with his usual joy and in many languages—German, Russian, English, Yiddish, and Hebrew. Even though everyone was there to remember something terrible, the light in Theo's heart and the wonderful music melted something inside of their hearts, and they felt a very special feeling, something holy. At the end, Theo asked everyone to stand, to honor the memory of every Jewish person—and all of the people—who had been killed. He said a prayer for the Austrian people, that they should always live in goodness and in peace. Then he said something important, something we must never forget.

"The mass murderers are gone," Theo said, his voice both soft and strong, "and I am still here, singing my people's songs of peace and freedom."

That night, we looked out the window at Vienna, lit up and glowing in the moonlight. Theo was quiet for some time and then said to me, his loving wife: "Everyone in this world is created for some purpose. Maybe it was for this day that God created me." And in the moment, I made a promise: to tell this story as many times as I could, to as many people as I could, for the rest of the days of my life.

Yiddish The Language of Theo's Childhood

As you read in this story, the boy spoke Yiddish with his papa. Yiddish was the language that all of the Jews in Central and Eastern Europe used to speak with each other. Even though most Jews could also speak the language of the countries they lived in, it was nice to have their own language so they could talk to each other whether they lived in Austria, Russia, Poland, Italy, France, or even Denmark or England. Anything you can think of, you could say it in Yiddish. Children played in Yiddish, parents cuddled and argued in Yiddish, people talked to their horses and cows and cats in Yiddish. They dreamed in Yiddish too! Yiddish is a beautiful language, with many funny sounding words and smart ways to say things. There were jokes, songs, movies, books, and newspapers, all in Yiddish.

Sadly, many of the people who spoke Yiddish died during the terrible war, or decided to forget it when they left or escaped from their homes. They were so upset about the things that had happened that they wanted to forget all about it and just start a new life.

Happily, not everybody forgot, and there are many people today who are trying to give the language a new life. Ask your parents or grandparents if they know any Yiddish. They will probably tell you that their parents only spoke it when they didn't want the children to understand. They probably do know at least a few words. Maybe your family can decide to learn some Yiddish together; then you can have your own secret language!

Here are just a few words to get you started. (Note: The *ch* is never hard as in "chin," but soft as in "Chanukah." The *a* is always like in "America," but *ay* makes a long *a* as in "may" or "ray.")

HELLO, HIYA	**Gutn tog**
GIRL	**May-dl**
BOY	**Yin-gl**
CHILDREN	**Kinder**
MOM	**Ma-meh**
DAD	**Ta-teh**

The boy called his bobeh Oma, which is German.

GRANDMA	**Bo-beh**
GRANDPA	**Zey-deh**
SISTER	**Zhves-ter**
BROTHER	**Bru-der**
FAMILY	**Mish-pu-che**
CAT	**Katz**
DOG	**Hoont**
BIRD	**Foy-gl**
CITY	**Shtot**
LIGHT	**Licht**
GAME	**Shpeel**
CAR	**Ma-sheen**
TV	**Teleh-viz-yeh**
MY NAME IS	**Mine nomen iz . . .**
OH NO!	**Oy vey!**
SO?	**Nu?**

DELICIOUS!	**Ge-shmak!**
DISGUSTING!	**Ekl-dik**
CRAZY	**Meh-shu-geh**
STOP PESTERING ME!	**Hok mir nit kayn chainik**
COMPLAIN	**Kvetch**
PLEASE	**Bit-teh**
THANK YOU	**A shaynem dank**
GOD BLESS YOU! (when you sneeze)	**Tsum gezunt**
I'M SORRY	**Ant-shul-dich**
I LOVE YOU	**Ich hob dir lib**
HAPPY CHANUKAH	**A fray-le-chen cha-ne-keh!**
GO TO SLEEP!	**Gay-shlofn**
GOOD NIGHT	**A guteh nacht**
GOODBYE!	**Zai-ge-zunt**
DREAM	**Cholem**

actually means Don't bang my teapot

—literally, be healthy

The numbers

1	**Ayn**
2	**Tsvay**
3	**Drey**
4	**Feer**
5	**Finf**
6	**Zeks**
7	**Zibm**
8	**Ocht**
9	**Neyn**
10	**Tzen**

Oma's Honey Cake (Lekach)

If you were ever to stand outside one of the bakeries of the City of Light and look in the window, you would surely lick your lips! Oh, how beautiful all of the pastries look, arranged so prettily in their cases. There are squares and triangles and little round towers, all covered with chocolate and buttercream and jellies, and decorated with fruit and powdered sugar. How could you possibly choose just one, or even two?

The most famous cake in Vienna is the *Sachertorte*, a delicious chocolate cake with a dark chocolate glaze and whipped cream. Many bakeries boast that their Sachertorte is the best one in the city; and some come in all kinds of fancy boxes, all wrapped up in nice paper and silk ribbons.

Some children were lucky enough to have an Oma who could bake cakes that tasted better than any you could buy in a bakery: anyway, we all know that things that are made with love taste better than anything money can buy. Theo's Oma knew how to bake many delicious pastries. Like many of the Jewish people in Vienna and all of Europe, Oma had a special cake that she made for Rosh Hashana (New Year) and for happy, wonderful days like Bar Mitzvahs or weddings. The Yiddish name for honey cake was *lekach*, which sounds like the German word *lecke*, which means lick.

Like most grandmothers of that time, Oma didn't use recipes when she cooked and baked: a *bissele'* (a little) of this, and a bissele' of that, and before long the whole house smelled like heaven.

Here is a recipe for Oma's honey cake. If you can resist, it will taste much better the next day (and even better the day after that!) so maybe taste one slice while it is warm, but keep the rest for tomorrow. To be like real Viennese people, eat your lekach with whipped cream on top.

Heat oven to 350 degrees. Butter the bottom of three loaf pans (5" x 8") or one cake pan (9"x 13"). If you have a tube pan (10") you could use that for a nice ring-shaped cake.

Dry Ingredients

- 3½ cups unbleached flour (up to half of the flour can be whole wheat)
- 2 tsp. baking powder
- 1 tsp. baking soda
- 4–5 tsp. cinnamon

- 1 tsp. pumpkin pie spice (or ½ tsp. nutmeg + ½ tsp. cloves)
- A pinch of salt

Wet Ingredients

- 3 eggs
- 1 cup butter, melted (or 1 cup vegetable oil)
- 1½ cups honey
- 1 cup brown sugar (if you like things very sweet, add an additional ¼ cup of white sugar)
- 1½ cups coffee
- 1 teaspoon vanilla
- slivered almonds

1. In a large bowl, combine the first six ingredients, maybe with a wooden spoon if you have one. Once everything is well mixed, make a big well in the middle.
2. Combine the wet ingredients in a separate bowl and pour into the well; mix until the batter looks smooth. Don't over beat, as this would make the cake dry.
3. Pour the batter into the buttered pan(s), sprinkle the slivered almonds on top, and bake in the oven until the middle feels solid and springs back a little when you touch it—about 45–55 minutes. (You can test for doneness at 45 minutes and let the cake(s) bake longer if needed, but be careful not to over bake. You will know the cake is almost ready when the kitchen fills with a delicious smell.)

Let the cake(s) cool down before slicing, and remember—lekach (honey cake) really does taste better the next day!

A Song to End the Book and Say Goodbye

Theo recorded this song especially for you, because he knew that some day you would be reading this book, and thinking about all of the things you learned. Theo felt that music was the best thing ever, and would sing a song when he was happy or sad or to laugh or say I'm sorry or to say goodbye. This song was written by Samuel Goldfarb and Samuel Grossman so long ago that Theo was just a tiny boy at the time. They also wrote the music for another song that you surely know: "I Have a Little Dreidel."

You can hear Theo sing this song if you go to theodorebikel.org/thecityoflight or momentmag.com/the cityoflight.

Little Candle Fires

By Samuel E. Goldfarb
and Samuel Grossman, 1927

From the album
Dreidel I Shall Play

Arranged and produced
by Craig Taubman

Performed by Theodore Bikel

On this night let us light
one little candle fire
What a sight, oh so bright
one little candle fire

1

On this night let us light
two little candle fires
What a sight, oh so bright
two little candle fires

On this night let us light
three little candle fires
What a sight, oh so bright
three little candle fires.

On this night, let us light
eight little candle fires
They say fight for the right
eight little candle fires
They say fight for the right
say little candle fires.

2 3 4 5 6 7 8

Acknowledgments

This little book you hold in your hands was born out of a short story written by Theodore Bikel z"l in 2014, at the request of our dear friend, Nadine Epstein, editor-in-chief and publisher of *Moment Magazine*. The original story was published in *Moment* and aired on NPR's "Chanukka Lights" program. When Nadine approached me about expanding the story into a book for Moment Books/Mandel Vilar Press, I was delighted. Without the patient, skillful direction of Robert Mandel, publisher and director of MVP, the story would not have grown into the full book it has come to be. Noah Phillips, our wonderful illustrator, has been delightful to work with. Anne Masters added her great talent to the cover. It was Barbara Werden, with her wealth of wisdom and experience, who pulled everything together, and our designer, Sophie Appel, who gave the book its beautiful look. My deep gratitude to all of you.

A heartfelt thank you to Craig Taubman for bringing the song "Little Candles" to Theo in his last months, for the beautiful recording, and for all of the light you bring. Thanks to Myron Gordon for graciously allowing us to use your father

Samuel E. Goldfarb's song in this book, and Peter Yarrow, brother of our hearts, for your early reading and endorsement. A *sheynem dank* to Miri Koral and Sam Norich for your gracious supervision of the Yiddish.

Thank you, Elka Ginsburg and Don Pequignot for your encouragement, enthusiasm, and wise counsel; and to my sons Zeev and Noam, for your love and support: as always, you were my first, and best, readers.

We will never forget the late Barbara Prammer, former President of the Austrian National Assembly, a gentlewoman, a visionary, and a true and powerful leader. May her memory be always for a blessing.

Theo Meir Bikel z"l led a beautiful and extraordinary life; the gifts he gave us are too many to count. He remembered the events in this book every day of his life, and he would have been tickled pink to see his story published in this form—a children's book! It was a profound and humbling honor to have been given the chance to commingle my words with his; just as it has been a humbling and almost unfathomable honor to commingle my life and my heart with his. My gratitude and love for my beloved husband truly knows no bounds—may his memory be a blessing forever and ever.

About the Contributors

Theodore Bikel (1924–2015) was an actor, singer, writer and social justice activist. His was a brilliant career, spanning more than 70 years. As an Oscar, Tony and Emmy nominated actor, he played Tevye in *Fiddler on the Roof* more than 2,000 times, and originated the role of Captain Von Trapp in the Broadway production of the *Sound of Music*. He had roles in many hit films such as *My Fair Lady*, *The Russians Are Coming* and the *African Queen*, and guest starred in almost every major TV show including *All in the Family*, *Star Trek*, *The Twilight Zone*, and *Law and Order*. As a musician, he recorded more than 20 best-selling albums, mainly in the folk genre, and Bikel's Yiddish recording are the best selling Yiddish albums of all time. Bikel was one of the founders of the Newport Folk Festival and was a central figure in the American folk revival movement. A devoted activist, he was deeply involved with the civil rights movement in the 60s and the 70s, in the efforts to free Soviet Jewry in the 70s and 80s.

Bikel was born in Vienna into a staunchly Socialist-Zionist family. Young Theo and his parents fled Austria after the Anschluss, settling in pre-independence Palestine. He studied Drama in the Royal Academy of the Dramatic Arts in London, achieving great success in West End theatre before moving to New York in 1957

Aimee Ginsburg Bikel is an American-Israeli writer, journalist, community organizer, and public speaker. A graduate of Hebrew University, she was an award-winning journalist and radio broadcaster in Israel before becoming the first full-time Israeli correspondent in India, a post she held for 15 years. She is the director of the Theodore Bikel Legacy Project, which she founded after her husband Theodore Bikel's passing in 2015.

Noah Phillips is a Brooklyn-based writer, illustrator, activist, and social worker. His artwork has appeared in magazines, newspapers and a book of children's stories called *The Three Chickens and Five Other Stories*.